TIMMY on the TOILET

Peta Lemon   Maria Dasic Todoric

This book is dedicated to toilets everywhere.
Who knows, maybe one day yours will fly too.

© 2017 Peta Lemon, Quirky Picture Press

Illustrations by Maria Dasic Todoric

**Quirky
Picture
Press**

Timmy was walking to school one day…

Timmy went over and, to his surprise,
a fairy was lying before his eyes.
The fairy was tangled inside the stack,
pitifully rolling around on her back.

Timmy bent down, unhooked her
wing and gently untangled
the poor little thing.

The fairy was free!

And, with a swish,
flew over to Timmy.

I grant you one wish.
Listen carefully to what I
say - your wish will come
true straight away.

The fairy then grinned and off she flew,
leaving Timmy to decide what to do.

What should he wish for?

His teacher, Miss Grobble, to sprout a big beard?

To slay a fierce dragon
as everyone cheered?

Timmy decided to choose after school.
"My wish will come true! This is so cool!"

Miss Grobble was waiting for him at the gate.
"Timmy!" She growled, "Why are you late?"
"Miss Grobble," He said, "I've just saved a fairy!"

"Nonsense!" She barked, sounding angry and scary.

"You horrible boy! Get out of my way.
I'm going to eat all your lunch today!"

Timmy walked on,
holding back tears.

Should he wish for
Miss Grobble to
have rabbit ears?

At break time Timmy went to the loo.
He still hadn't decided what he would do.

He looked out
the window.

A bird flew by.

"How nice that looks.
I wish I could fly."

"Oh no!" He gasped, "That was a mistake.
That isn't the wish I wanted to make!"
But it was too late – his wish had been made.
The toilet creaked… and wobbled… and swayed…..

Then rose completely up from the floor.

And flew right out of the bathroom door!

Down the corridor, past all the classes.
Miss Grobble thought she needed new glasses.

It buzzed round the school – then whooshed outside.
"Timmy's flying on the toilet!"
His school friends cried.

They all piled out to watch him fly
and loop the loop up in the sky.
Timmy was having wonderful fun....

.... Until someone said,

"We can all see your bum!"

"Stop!" Exclaimed Timmy, "Put me down!"

The loo didn't stop
but headed to town.

It flew past the shop where he bought his treats.
Toys, games and occasionally sweets.

It zoomed past his gran
who was out having tea.

And narrowly missed
hitting a tree.

"Make this thing stop!" He started yelling.
"I should be in class doing my spelling!"

But the toilet kept going – this time to the train.
"Put me down please!" He bellowed in vain.

The ladies and gents were taking their seats,
when Timmy came screeching down one of the streets.
They jumped to their feet and stood there aghast,
as Timmy whizzed past them ever so fast.

"I should be at school learning to read!"
Now the toilet was steadily gathering speed.

He caught up with some geese
and gave them a race.

And looked like a rocket
shooting through space.

Timmy's flight finally came to an end
when he tipped off the edge as he went round a bend.

He landed head first
in a haystack
and felt someone gently
tugging his back.

He got to his feet and, to his surprise,
the fairy was flying before his eyes.

Thanks to you the whole town has laughed. I grant you a wish for looking so daft!

He thought for a moment and scratched his head,
grinning widely, before he said.
"My wish is that everyone flies on the loo.
It really was fun – they must try it too."

His wish was then granted and soon the whole town
was flying around on their loos up and down.
Everyone had wonderful fun
but couldn't believe what Timmy had done.

Back at the school, with a munch and a crunch,
Miss Grobble was eating a little girl's lunch.
She chomped through her sandwich as the girl cried,
and the loo came swooping in from the side.

And scooped up Miss Grobble,
who didn't enjoy her ride on the loo,

"You horrible boy!"

Then with
a bounce
and a bump
and a shake....

Miss Grobble plunged into a fishing lake.

As Timmy's wish slowly faded away,
the toilets all landed and, to this day…

He's remembered for making the whole town fly.
Now they smile at his statue as they pass by.

In this town
in 2018
Timmy made
everyone fly
on their toilets.

Printed in Great
Britain
by Amazon

31346111R00022